unraveling
Rose

written by Brian Wray   illustrated by Shiloh Penfield

Schiffer Publishing Ltd®

4880 Lower Valley Road • Atglen, PA 19310

Other Schiffer Books on Related Subjects:

Baby Blue Has the Blues, K.I. Al-Ghan, Illustrations by Haitham Al-Ghani,
978-0-7643-3732-1
Bertie Bumble Bee: Troubled by the Letter "b", K.I. Al-Ghani, Illustrations by Haitham Al-Ghani,
978-0-7643-3993-6
Ronnie Raven Recycles, K.I. Al-Ghani, , Illustrations by Haitham Al-Ghani,
978-0-7643-3840-3

Library of Congress Control Number: 2017935415

Cover design by Brenda McCallum
Type set in Love Letters/Book Antiqua

ISBN: 978-0-7643-5393-2
Printed in China

Co-published by Pixel Mouse House &
Schiffer Publishing, Ltd.
4880 Lower Valley Road
Atglen, PA 19310
Phone: (610) 593-1777; Fax: (610) 593-2002
E-mail: Info@schifferbooks.com
Web: www.schifferbooks.com

For our complete selection of fine books on this and related subjects,
please visit our website at www.schifferbooks.com. You may also write for a free catalog.

Schiffer Publishing's titles are available at special discounts for bulk purchases for sales promotions or premiums. Special editions, including personalized covers, corporate imprints, and excerpts, can be created in large quantities for special needs. For more information, contact the publisher.

We are always looking for people to write books on new and related subjects.
If you have an idea for a book, please contact us at proposals@schifferbooks.com.

For everyone who took the time to sit down with me and read a story, nurturing my imagination. And to my children, Catherine and Sylvia, who've shown me what having an imagination is all about.

~ B.W.

To my parents, thanks for all the pencils and paper growing up.

~ S.P.

Rose was sewn together with love.

She was named for the color of her flannel cheeks. She could have been named Cotton for her tail or Floppy for her long ears.

But Rose was named Rose and she liked that.

Rose loved the little boy who hugged her tightly
at bedtime.

She loved when the little boy climbed trees with her, or tossed her high in the air and caught her.

But Rose's most favorite thing was reading stories with the boy.

It was her job to turn the pages, and Rose loved that.

Life was just the way she wanted it, and Rose did everything she could to keep it that way.

If the books on the shelf weren't straight, Rose wanted to straighten them.

At tea time, Rose made sure all the tea cups' handles pointed to the right.

And there wasn't a single wrinkle on her polka dot dress. Rose made sure that everything was perfect.

Then, one sunny Sunday morning, Rose discovered — just under her left arm — a tiny loose thread, dangling free.

"Well, that shouldn't be there," she thought.

Knowing that the little loose thread was dangling,
Rose found it hard to concentrate on painting
a picture . . .

. . . on building towers with her blocks . . .

. . . or even on reading stories with the boy.

That loose thread was all she could think about.

Finally, Rose had to fix it. Pinching the thread firmly, she pulled. But it didn't come out.

The thread just got longer.

When she tugged again,
the thread kept coming
and opened up a tiny hole.
Rose could see a gap
of white stuffing.

"Oh no," Rose sighed.

So the stuffed bunny left the
thread alone . . . for a time.

But it didn't take long before the thought of that dangling thread filled her mind. And Rose pulled at it again. And again. And again. And again.

And the string grew longer. And the little hole where she could see her white stuffing grew larger.

Rose tried to hide the length of string in the pocket of her dress. She was embarrassed by what she was doing, and she didn't want anybody to see.

Still, Rose couldn't stop.

Now when the boy tossed her in the air,
Rose was worried that the ball of thread would
tumble from her pocket.

Still, Rose couldn't stop pulling the thread.

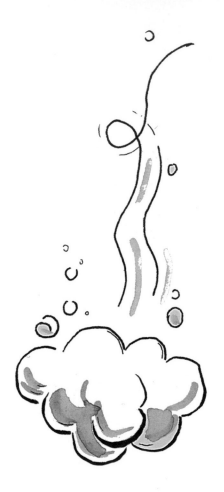

She kept pulling at the thread until her arm started to really unravel and some of the stuffing fell out.

Rose put on a sweater to cover the hole,
but her left arm wouldn't work at all.
Nearly all the stuffing was gone.

She didn't want to paint pictures anymore. Or climb trees. But worst of all, without both of her hands, Rose couldn't turn pages.

When the boy asked if she wanted to read stories together, Rose sadly shook her head no.

That one unraveling thread kept Rose
from doing the things she loved most.

She needed to make a big change.

Rose put back her stuffing, threaded a needle,
and — stitch-by-stitch — carefully sewed herself together.

When she was finished and the hole was fixed,
that little loose thread was still dangling.

And that was okay. With practice, Rose forgot the thread was there. The more she didn't pull, the more she didn't have to pull—the more she and the boy could read their stories together.

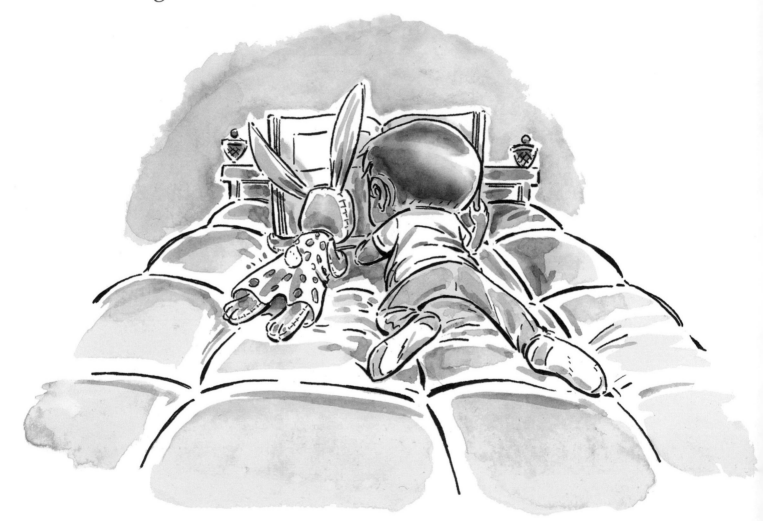

The more she understood that things don't always have to be perfect . . .

. . . the more room there was in Rose's head to do the things she loved and to feel loved.

about the
creators

Brian has been writing professionally since 2003, when he was awarded the Nicholl Fellowship in Screenwriting by the Academy of Motion Picture Arts & Sciences. Since then, he has written for Walt Disney Studios, and has earned a variety of television producing and writing credits. Brian is inspired by his time at Disney and the bottomless imagination of his daughters.

Shiloh's previous work includes *Boy Zero* for Caliber Comics, a guest artist spot on *Red Knight* published by Dead West Comics, and multiple independent projects. Located in Brooklyn, her calico cat, Maki, maintains quality control and ensures all pages are delivered on time.

a word about
OBSESSIVE COMPULSIVE DISORDER

Many children struggle to overcome anxiety. Roughly three percent of children in the United States alone are affected by Obsessive Compulsive Disorder (OCD).

A child with OCD suffers from compulsions and obsessions that can interfere with everyday life. A child may have a persistent fear of germs or vomiting that they can't ignore. In school, children who feel the need for perfection may compulsively go back to re-check their work, whether repeatedly reading sentences aloud, or double and triple checking their math work.

However, thanks to advances in research, we are discovering that there are ways to help. Outside of therapy, parents and teachers have a powerful and important role in helping children struggling with OCD. Research shows that when parents are involved, it improves the effects of treatment.

Here are just four examples of how grown-ups can help with coping techniques at home and in school.

- Parents naturally want to shield their children from things that bring on anxieties associated with their OCD. However, exposing the child to fears in a systemized, step-by-step way can help manage those fears. For children with a fear of germs, adults may encourage the child to use door knobs or pick up something dirty and not wash their hands.

- To avoid disruptive behavior in the classroom or embarrassment for the child, teachers can work out a system of non-verbal communication, allowing a student who feels symptoms of OCD coming on to quietly notify the teacher. This gives the student an opportunity to either go to a predetermined safe place in the classroom or leave the classroom altogether if necessary.

- Some children with OCD seek relief from their obsessive thoughts by performing specific rituals, believing that those rituals will prevent something "bad" from happening. Help a child to see OCD as a bully, even giving it a name. To change the ritual, encourage the child to challenge the OCD. For example, "Try telling 'the OCD' that today you're going to put on the left shoe before the right shoe."

- It is not uncommon for children with OCD to be bullied in school, because of their symptoms. Teachers can speak to the class, explaining to children what OCD is and allowing the child suffering with OCD to be part of the discussion. Giving them a chance to talk about their specific issues can help alleviate confusion for classmates and embarrassment for the child.

With the appropriate treatment and coping techniques, a child suffering with OCD can better manage their symptoms, allowing them to begin enjoying a life less controlled by obsessive and compulsive thoughts.

For more information, please visit the Child Mind Institute at www.childmind.org and search "OCD."